P9-DDH-908

MORNINGSIDE ELEM. SCHOOL
SALEM, OREGON

GRAHAM CRACKER ANIMALS 1–2–3

by NANCY WHITE CARLSTROM

illustrated by JOHN SANDFORD

Macmillan Publishing Company   New York

Salem-Keizer Public Schools   DUP
3 0245 0000 0098 9

Text copyright © 1989 by Nancy White Carlstrom
Illustrations copyright © 1989 by John Sandford
All rights reserved. No part of this book may be reproduced or
transmitted in any form or by any means, electronic or mechanical,
including photocopying, recording, or by any information storage and
retrieval system, without permission in writing from the Publisher.
Macmillan Publishing Company
866 Third Avenue, New York, NY 10022
Collier Macmillan Canada, Inc.
Printed and bound in Singapore   First American Edition

10 9 8 7 6 5 4 3 2 1

The text of this book is set in 12 point Weidemann Book.
The illustrations are rendered in pen-and-ink
with airbrush and watercolored dyes.

Library of Congress Cataloging-in-Publication Data
Carlstrom, Nancy White.
Graham cracker animals 1-2-3/by Nancy White Carlstrom;
illustrated by John Sandford.—1st American ed.   p.   cm.
Summary: A collection of poems following the activities
of preschoolers as they play, bathe, prepare
for bedtime, and explore the world around them.
ISBN 0-02-717270-8
1. Children's poetry, American. [1. American poetry.]
I. Sandford, John, date, ill. II. Title.
PS3553.A7355G7 1989   811'.54—dc 19
88-13434 CIP AC

To JOSHUA WHITE CARLSTROM

These rhymes are for you
with my love too.
And please share
with Madelyn Claire,
your cousin Maddy from Rochester.

—N.W.C.

For ELEANOR LOUISE,

my graham cracker animal,
with love
from Papa

—J.S.

GRAHAM CRACKER ANIMALS 1–2–3

Graham Cracker Animals
1–2–3,

Marching in a straight line
Marching to the sea.

Graham Cracker Animals
Here's one more,

Following the others
Now there are four.

Graham Cracker Animals
All climbing up,

Dancing in a circle
Around my blue cup.

Graham Cracker Animals
On a white sea,

Sailing in a silver spoon
Coming home to me.

Graham Cracker Animals
Slipping in a rush,

Tumble in the milky deep
Graham Cracker Mush.

RIDE, RIDE, RIDE

Ride on Daddy's shoulders
Ride on Granny's knee,

Ride the horse to Portland
For apple bread and tea.

Drive the little *putt-putt*
Down the hilly steep,

Watch out for the growly bears
Watch out for the sheep.

Sail the laundry basket
Sail it out to sea,

Don't forget to wave the flag
Wave the flag for me.

Fly your cardboard box plane
Zoom it through the sky,

Fly it over mountains
Fly it fast and high.

Chugalug the chair train
Chug it down the track,

See you later, Baby
But please come back!

PLAY, PLAY, PLAY

Bang on the kettle
Beat on the pan,

Mix Mama's muffins
Stir in the bran.

Throw down the raisins
Listen to them plop,

Pour the molasses
Brown, sticky drops.

Clang with the pot lids
Ping with the spoons,

Roll out the cookie dough
Cut little moons.

Pound out the pizza
Toss in the air,

Squeeze, please, and pinch it
Flour everywhere.

Play a song of baking
Busy little hands,

Making merry music
In the kitchen band.

ME, ME, ME

One face, two eyes, one nose
One head with hair that grows

Two ears to hear you say
I love you. Let's go play.

A mouth to talk
I say bye-bye

Sometimes I laugh
Sometimes I cry.

Two strong arms
To hug my bear

When we sit
On my blue chair.

Two hands to hold
When we go out

Two legs to walk
And run about.

Many children
Everywhere I see

Many others
But just one me.

SHOES, SHOES, SHOES

Old shoes, new shoes
Hop-into shoes

Quiet, hushing, tiptoe shoes
Loud, stomping, clomping shoes

Dancing, prancing, skipping shoes
Jumping, bumping, tripping shoes

Shoes in a heap
Sitting on the floor

Shoes in a line
Marching out the door

Soft, stay-at-home shoes
High, walk-alone shoes

Mixed-up shoes for Daddy
Mommy, and my brother

Find the go-together shoes
One shoe needs the other

Brother's running-fast shoes
Daddy's buckle-tight shoes
Mommy's slip-in right shoes

I've found the tiny tie shoes
My shoes, my shoes.

HATS, HATS, HATS

One hat, two hats
Peekaboo hats

Old hats, new hats
See right through hats

Soft, fuzzy, furry hats
Swish, in-a-hurry hats

Yard hats, hard hats
Hats that flap

Ski hats, tree hats
Hats that snap

Hats with tassels
Hats with feathers

Hats to wear
In rainy weather

Hats for cold
Hats for shade

Hats in stores
And hats homemade

Hats in closets
Hats on beds

Match up hats
They all need heads.

POCKETS, POCKETS, POCKETS

Pockets for rocks
And pieces of string

Pockets for buttons
And round whirly things

Pockets for papers
And tiny toy cars

Pockets for stickers
Three small shiny stars

Pockets for pennies
And marbles for shaking

Pockets for feathers
And fuzzy nest making

Pockets for hands
To hide from the cold

Pushing and poking
Now pockets with holes

Holes growing bigger
And if we don't sew

Tell me please
Where will these
Pocket things go?

APPLES, APPLES, APPLES

Big apple, little apple
Growing on the tree

One apple in my hand
It's for me

Biting, chewing
Baking, stewing

In a sauce
In a pie

Apples on my pancakes
Stacked up high.

Shiny apples, round apples
Falling on the ground apples

Green apple, yellow apple
Apple, apple red

Apple dapple dumpling
Standing on my head

Upside down
And inside out

High apples, sky apples
Apples all about.

WHEELS, WHEELS, WHEELS

Big cars, brown cars
Rolling through the town cars

Big trucks, white trucks
Rolling through the night trucks

Big trains, black trains
Rolling on the track trains

Car wheels, truck wheels
Wheels on trains

Rolling in the sunshine
Rolling in the rain

Round and round
Fast and slow

Wheels are rolling
There they go

Rolling along
Singing a song

Zoom brr-room
Zoom brr-room

Wheels, wheels, wheels.

BIRTHDAY, BIRTHDAY, BIRTHDAY

Balloons on the ceiling
Balloons on the floor

Hoppy-poppy birthday
Hoppy-pop some more.

Candles on the big cake
Candles on the floor

Huffy-puffy birthday
Huffy-puff some more.

Icing on my fingers
Icing on the floor

Sticky-licky birthday
Sticky-lick some more.

Ice cream on my new shirt
Ice cream on the floor

Slippy-drippy birthday
Slippy-drip some more.

Presents on the table
Presents on the floor

Happy-snappy birthday
Happy-snap some more.

HIDING, HIDING, HIDING

Feet in socks
And feet in shoes,

Feet are hiding
Two by two.

Sometimes toes come
Peeking through.

Heads in hats
Are hiding too.

They hide from rain
They hide from snow,

Or they don't need
A place to go.

They hide at home
When they're at play,

A different hat
A different day.

Shoes and hats
To name a few,

Hide in boxes
I can too.

You see my hat
You see my shoes,

I close my eyes
I can't see you.

Hiding, hiding, hiding!

WATER, WATER, WATER

Hot water, cold water
Very hard to hold water

Slip from my fingers
Drip off my nose

Run down my back
And trickle through my toes.

Bubbles, bubbles, watch them float
With the sponges and a boat

Can you find the sinking soap?
It's squishy squashy soft.

Water splashing in the tub
Water spilling on the floor

Look at me, I'll pull the plug
Gush, rush, roar.

Water spinning round and round
I get up as it goes down

Yellow duck does flip-flops
I shake off my drip drops

Wet is what you always get
In the water.

SILLY, SILLY, SILLY

Silly-willy you
Silly-willy me,

Lift your two arms in the air
Tickle-wickle whee.

Silly-willy goose
Silly-willy cat,

Put your pj's on your head
Wear them like a hat.

Silly-willy dog
Silly-willy bear,

Hold your hands behind your back
Now let down your hair.

Silly-willy me
Silly-willy you,

Hide under your blanket
Play some peekaboo.

Silly-willy book
Silly-willy clown,

Silly-willy, can you sleep?
Standing upside down.

SLEEP, SLEEP, SLEEP

Hugs and kisses
Cuddles three

Twirl around
And dance with me.

Clap your hands
And tap your feet

Nibble nibble
You're so sweet.

Snuggle closer
Snuggle near

Whisper secrets
In my ear.

Talking softly
Rocking slow

Off to dreamland
Off you go.

Sleep my darling
Sleep my dove

Dream in peace
And wake with love.